DON'T BUTT IN

HEATH McKENZIE

A Scholastic Press book from Scholastic Australia

FOR ALL THE PARENTS

whose kids promptly went 'butt out' after reading the last book!
Hopefully this book makes amends . . . butt it probably won't.

Scholastic Press
An imprint of Scholastic Australia Pty Limited (ABN 11 000 614 577)
PO Box 579 Gosford NSW 2250
www.scholastic.com.au

Part of the Scholastic Group
Sydney · Auckland · New York · Toronto · London · Mexico City
· New Delhi · Hong Kong · Buenos Aires · Puerto Rico

Published by Scholastic Australia in 2019.
Text and illustrations copyright © Heath McKenzie, 2019.

Heath McKenzie asserts his moral rights as the author and illustrator of this work.

 A catalogue record for this
book is available from the
National Library of Australia

ISBN: 978-1-76066-559-3

Typeset in Agnes by Hand and Lovage.

Heath McKenzie created these illustrations digitally.

Printed and bound by TWP Sdn Bhd, Malaysia.
Scholastic Australia's policy, in association with Tien Wah Press, is to use papers that are
renewable and made efficiently from wood grown in responsibly managed forests, so as to
minimise its environmental footprint.

10 9 8 7 6 5 4 3 2 1   19 20 21 22 23 / 1

TODAY FEELS LIKE A **GOOD DAY** TO TRY SOMETHING **NEW . . .**

PANTS!

I WON'T BUTT OUT, I'LL BUTT IN!

May I please have
one pair of—

Do you know when the bus
will arrive—

Let's all give a big cheer—

PPY **BU**TT **ID**AY

FOR MY
REAR
IN THIS
GEAR!

Hey BUDDY!
Get your butt out of—

All right now, everybody say—

Your new pants will be—

BUTTRAGEOUSLY
BUTT-
NORMOUS!

EXCUSE ME!

That's QUITE enough of your cheek! It's very rude to interrupt when someone is speaking! Please don't—

DON'T WHAT?